THANKFUL HEARTS AND PUMPKIN SPICE KISSES

- THEY'RE FORCED TO SAVE THANKSGIVING TOGETHER — AND ACCIDENTALLY FALL IN LOVE

EMMA LANE

CONTENTS

About the Author   v

1. Pie Problems   1
2. Stuffing & Sass   5
3. Pumpkin Patch Plans   9
4. Battle of the Side Dishes   13
5. Kitchen Fires and Flashbacks   17
6. The Great Pie-Off   21
7. Whisked Away   24
8. Past Its Expiration Date   28
9. Cornbread & Confessions   32
10. The Fallout   36
11. Friendsgiving Fail?   39
12. The Night Before   43
13. Main Street Magic   48
14. Pumpkin Spice Kisses   52
15. Second Helpings   56
16. Thankful Hearts   59
17. Thank you for reading!   62

About the Author

Emma Lane is back with her signature blend of small-town charm, slow-burn romance, and just the right dash of cinnamon. A lifelong believer that love stories are best served warm — preferably with pie — Emma wrote *Thankful Hearts and Pumpkin Spice Kisses* as a tribute to her favorite season, the power of found family, and the unexpected sweetness of second chances. Following the success of her debut, Home for the Holidays, Emma continues to craft stories full of cozy kitchens, stubborn hearts, and the kind of magic that only happens when the leaves start to turn. When she's not writing, she's thrifting for fall décor, testing pie recipes she'll never perfect, and plotting her next seasonal romance — always with a vintage mug in hand.

CHAPTER 1
PIE PROBLEMS

It was the kind of autumn morning that felt like a promise.

The air was honey-crisp and golden, every tree dressed like it had somewhere to be, and Claire Monroe was certain that if magic were ever to happen, it would happen in a town like this — under a canopy of amber leaves, with a pumpkin spice latte warming her hand and a Taylor Swift remix pulsing from her car speakers.

Harvest Hollow welcomed her like a postcard: cobblestone streets, wreaths on doors, hand-lettered chalkboards outside coffee shops boasting phrases like *Give Thanks & Eat Pie*. It was everything she hoped for, everything she needed — not just for her blog, *The Whiskered Life*, but for herself. After a long year of deadlines, breakups, and a soul-sucking LA summer, she craved something *real*.

"This is it, Whiskers," she said, speaking to both her audience and her phone camera, perched dashboard-style. "We made it. Fall heaven. Population: me. And maybe a couple dozen pies."

She flashed a grin, adjusted her favorite burnt-orange beanie, and kept recording as she rolled into the fairgrounds where the **Harvest Hollow Thanksgiving Food Festival** was supposed to be in full swing.

Only... it wasn't.

Claire blinked. Slowed. Parked.

There were no booths. No wafts of turkey legs or cinnamon cider. No flannel-clad locals laughing over pie tastings. Just two volunteers sitting on a hay bale, looking like they were waiting for a bus that forgot them.

And one sign. One damning, hideous, ridiculous sign:

"Venue Closed Due to Booking Conflict. Festival Postponed. Happy Thanksgiving!"

Claire stared. Blinked again. "No. Nope. This is a joke, right?"

She got out of the car, latte sloshing in hand, and stormed up to the sign, as if proximity might make it make sense.

"Excuse me?" she called to the volunteers, voice pitched somewhere between cheerful and *verging on meltdown*. "Where's the festival?"

"Supposed to be here," said one teen with a shrug. "But I guess the wrestling match took priority."

"Wrestling match?" she echoed, blinking like her lashes might swat the nonsense away.

"Yup. Turkey Takedown. Town hall mix-up. Mayor Langford's already catching heat."

Claire stood frozen for a beat. Then she did what she always did when the world unraveled:

She hit *record*.

"Hello, lovely whisk-takers," she said into the lens with an almost-impressive amount of calm. "Live update from Harvest Hollow, where it appears Thanksgiving is currently... canceled? You're not going to *believe* what I just found—"

She spun the camera to the sign, then back to her face. "But don't worry. Yours truly is on the case."

And with that, Claire marched toward **Town Hall**, latte in one hand, camera in the other, and absolutely no plan besides *making someone explain how you cancel Thanksgiving.*

. . .

Town Hall smelled like old wood, cinnamon potpourri, and bureaucracy.

Claire barely registered the confused receptionist as she flung open the office door to Mayor Langford's office, only to immediately interrupt what sounded like a full-blown argument.

"No," a deep, gravelly voice was saying, "you can't just slap a turkey sticker on a wrestling mat and call it a festival, Langford."

Claire froze. Two pairs of eyes turned toward her. One belonged to a red-faced mayor who looked like he'd aged ten years in ten days. The other…

Well, the other belonged to a man who looked like autumn had decided to turn itself into a human: flannel shirt, rolled sleeves, dark eyes, even darker mood. If brooding were an Olympic sport, this man had medals.

"Oh," she said brightly, smoothing her coat. "Am I interrupting your rage meeting, or may I file my own complaint?"

The man turned. Took her in — beanie, boots, latte, and all.

"And you are?" he asked, voice rough like he used it more to curse at ovens than hold polite conversation.

"Claire Monroe. Food blogger. Festival ambassador. Emotional support pie enthusiast. And you are?"

"Eli Hunter. Chef. Local. Not interested."

Claire blinked. "Wow. Did you major in charm, or is this just raw talent?"

Mayor Langford sighed, rubbing his temples. "Claire, Eli — you've both clearly got opinions. Congratulations. You now have something in common."

"I don't think we do," Claire muttered.

"Oh, I'm pretty sure we do," Eli said, eyes narrowing. "You're one of those TikTok pie girls, aren't you?"

Claire gasped. "Excuse me?"

"You know the type. Pretty frosting. Zero depth. All whipped cream, no substance."

Claire bristled. "Well, Chef Frownypants, some of us believe food should be *fun*. Accessible. Joyful."

Eli smirked. "And some of us believe it should be edible."

"Enough!" the mayor barked. "This festival is on life support, and frankly, you two are the only ones who seem to care it's dying. So guess what?"

They both turned toward him.

He leaned forward, grinning like a man who just handed off a ticking time bomb.

"You're co-chairing the new version. Scaled down. Local. On a three-day deadline."

Claire blinked. "What."

Eli scowled. "No."

"Yes," the mayor said, already scribbling on a notepad. "Because if you don't, this town loses one of its biggest events of the year. And I get pitchforked by the pumpkin farmers."

Silence.

Claire looked at Eli. Eli looked at Claire. Her latte had gone cold. His glare had not.

"Fine," Claire said at last, tightening her grip on her phone. "But I'm warning you now — I'm allergic to grumpy."

Eli crossed his arms. "And I'm allergic to glitter. So let's hope your personality doesn't shed."

Mayor Langford exhaled as if releasing a long-held breath. "Well, seeing as you both care so much — congratulations. You're now in charge of saving Thanksgiving."

Claire sighed.

Eli muttered something about stuffing.

And somewhere outside, a turkey gobbled like it knew this was going to be *chaos*.

CHAPTER 2
STUFFING & SASS

It was the kind of disaster only a small town could spin into a punchline.

Thanksgiving had been canceled — *postponed*, technically — to make room for a wrestling match called "The Turkey Takedown." And somehow, Claire Monroe and a flannel-clad man with a knife-sharp glare were now the only thing standing between Harvest Hollow and total holiday humiliation.

Claire was still reeling.

"I'm sorry," she said for the third time, gripping the edge of the mayor's desk. "You're telling me a bunch of people in turkey-themed spandex took our venue?"

Mayor Langford cleared his throat, refusing to meet her eyes. "It's a beloved tradition."

"It's a crime against gravy," Claire snapped.

Eli leaned against the wall like he'd rather be anywhere else — preferably in a burning building with fewer opinions. "It's also done. So unless you've got a time machine, maybe stop arguing with reality."

Claire shot him a look. "I'm not arguing. I'm…processing."

"You process *loudly*."

Mayor Langford cut in, raising his voice over the bickering. "What we need is a quick, focused solution. A *scaled-down* version of the festival. Pop-ups, booths, maybe a live demo or two. Enough to save the spirit of it — and my inbox."

Claire opened her mouth to protest. Eli beat her to it.

"I'm not hosting a food circus," he said flatly. "If this town wants me to cook, I'll cook. Real food. Not whatever trend just went viral on a brunch board."

Claire folded her arms, eyes blazing. "Food can be fun and meaningful, Chef Frownypants. I happen to believe people connect over the simple stuff. Nostalgia. Warmth. Mini pumpkin hand pies."

Eli stared at her, unimpressed. "You mean sugar and a filter?"

"Excuse me?"

"Let me guess — your Thanksgiving memories come with a curated hashtag."

Claire's cheeks flushed. "And yours come with a side of judgment and thyme?"

Mayor Langford, bless him, looked like he was about to fake a heart attack just to escape the room.

THE MEETING that followed was less a planning session and more a polite war zone.

They sat in the town hall conference room, a whiteboard between them and a pot of over-steeped tea no one dared touch. Claire's side of the board bloomed with colorful ideas — food trucks shaped like turkeys, cider tasting corners, a "Stuffing Smackdown" cook-off. Eli's half was precise and minimal — one elegant layout for a long, communal harvest table with courses plated and timed.

Claire loved it. Hated it. Wanted to smudge it just to see if he'd blink.

They argued about signage (*Claire wanted chalkboard menus with little drawings; Eli wanted "legible fonts"*), timing (*she liked the idea of staggered tasting slots; he preferred one unified feast*), and tone (*she wanted cozy chaos, he wanted calm and curated*).

"You know," Claire muttered, circling a heart on her sketch of the cider stand, "not everything has to be so serious. It's pie. Not open-heart surgery."

Eli didn't look up from his notes. "I take both very seriously."

STILL, something shifted as the day wore on.

Claire caught Eli pausing to fix a crooked banner on the mayor's welcome board — not with irritation, but instinct. And when she brought up incorporating local high school volunteers, he didn't grumble. He just said, "As long as they wash their hands."

She noticed how focused he was. How his hands moved when he talked about pacing a meal. How even his grumpiness felt... rooted. Like there was a reason he was all edges.

And Eli — though he'd never admit it — began to wonder what hid behind Claire's constant smile. Not the curated kind. The one that cracked when she thought no one was watching. The one that slipped when she stared out the window for just a second too long.

She laughed loudly. Talked fast. Sparkled. But sometimes, he saw her go quiet.

It made him itch with questions he didn't want to ask.

AS THEY WRAPPED the third hour of negotiations and Claire's third cookie from the complimentary plate, the tension shifted again — just slightly.

Claire stood, brushing crumbs off her cardigan, and stuck out her hand. "Okay, Chef. Truce?"

Eli looked at her hand like it might bite him. Then — slowly — he shook it. His grip was warm and firm, and she refused to feel flustered by it.

"Let's just get through this," he muttered.

Claire smiled, wide and bright and full of mischief. "You're lucky I'm very charming under pressure."

He raised an eyebrow. "That's what I'm afraid of."

Outside the town hall, the wind picked up, scattering a swirl of leaves in gold and rust. Claire pulled her coat tighter and looked back at the building. Somewhere in there, her least favorite person just became her partner.

And Thanksgiving? Well, it wasn't canceled after all.

But it might be *completely unhinged*.

CHAPTER 3
PUMPKIN PATCH PLANS

Some ideas bloom quietly. Others arrive with the sound of boots crunching through leaves and a woman waving a map with jam on the corner.

Claire Monroe burst through the back door of Eli's restaurant like a cinnamon-scented hurricane, cheeks pink with excitement, her to-go latte trailing steam.

"I have an idea," she announced, in the same tone one might use for *I've just discovered time travel* or *there's a baby goat in the car*.

Eli didn't look up from the tray of root vegetables he was roasting. "That sentence never ends well."

"No, listen!" Claire skidded to a stop, cheeks flushed, waving a flyer. "Maple Acres. It's perfect. Lucy Carmichael — we went to middle school together — she owns the farm now. They've got a barn, a working kitchen, a pumpkin patch, and—bonus—the space is *free*."

Eli glanced at her over the edge of his glasses, unimpressed. "You want to move the entire festival to a farm?"

"Yes!" Claire chirped. "It's rustic. Authentic. Pinterest would weep with joy. Plus, lanterns in the barn rafters? A cider stand by the pumpkin patch? Come *on*, this is the content dream."

He blinked. "It smells like hay and regrets."

Claire gasped. "You culinary buzzkill."

"I'm not a buzzkill," he said. "I'm realistic."

"You're allergic to joy," she said, pulling out her phone. "Come on. Site visit. Now. If I have to suffer through your minimalist signage, you can handle some corn stalks."

Maple Acres looked like autumn had exploded, then politely tidied itself into perfection.

The barn stood tall and warm, wood aged to a perfect golden gray. The pumpkin patch stretched wide behind it, dotted with orange like someone had spilled a basket of suns. Kids ran through it with sticky fingers and tiny boots, laughter trailing behind them like ribbons.

Claire beamed. "Tell me this isn't magic."

Eli stepped out of the car and squinted. "It's…orange."

"You're impossible."

He followed her reluctantly across the gravel drive, hands in his jacket pockets. Claire bounced ahead like this was a scene from her childhood dreams — which, if she was being honest, it kind of was. Lucy came out to greet them, all hugs and flannel and "Oh my gosh, look at you!"

Claire introduced Eli with a too-cheerful, "This is Eli, our resident grinch. But don't worry, he's harmless unless exposed to whimsy."

Lucy grinned. "Perfect. We'll have him apple-bobbing by sunset."

Eli muttered something that sounded like a vow of silence and followed them inside.

The barn was…charming.

Even Eli couldn't deny that. The rafters were wide and strong, the space open and welcoming. Claire could already *see* it — the long tables with mismatched chairs, the glow of fairy lights, the laughter echoing off wood beams. It wasn't just an event space.

It felt like a beginning.

But when she turned to gauge Eli's reaction, he was inspecting a bale of hay like it had personally offended him.

"It'll take work," he said flatly. "The flooring's uneven. The lighting's bad. And don't get me started on food safety."

Claire sighed, hands on hips. "Why do I feel like you won't be satisfied unless everything smells like sourdough and existential despair?"

He didn't answer. Just turned away, arms crossed — and yet... he didn't walk off.

Outside, the sun began to dip into gold.

Claire found herself chatting with a group of kids near the patch, helping them guess the weight of a particularly round pumpkin. She laughed as one of them announced, "It's definitely ten thousand pounds."

Eli watched from a distance, leaning against the barn door. He didn't smile — not really — but something softened around his eyes. She was different when she wasn't trying. Less sparkle, more soul.

When Claire caught him watching, she didn't tease him.

Instead, they stood side by side, quiet for once, watching as the last rays of sunlight set the field on fire. The wind lifted Claire's hair. Eli's shoulders eased, just slightly.

It wasn't a romantic moment.

But it could have been.

Later, in the car, silence stretched long and full between them.

The road back into town curled through trees the color of cider and maple syrup, and neither of them spoke for a while — not out of tension, but something gentler. Like they were both afraid words might ruin the spell.

Claire's phone buzzed. She glanced at the screen and frowned.

A voice message from **Logan**, her ex-business partner, slid across the top.

"Claire. Call me. I've got something big. We might finally have our shot at a network deal. Think holiday pilot. Think L.A. Think soon."

She didn't press play. Just stared at the screen a moment too long.

Then she tucked it away and looked out the window.

"I know you hate this idea," she said quietly, watching the leaves dance past. "But… it feels right. Doesn't it?"

Eli didn't answer right away. Then, with a sigh, he murmured, "I don't hate it."

Claire turned to look at him.

"I just hate that you're probably right."

CHAPTER 4
BATTLE OF THE SIDE DISHES

S ome wars are waged with swords. Others with whispers. But in Harvest Hollow, the fiercest battle of the year began with a casserole dish and a passive-aggressive note on a community bulletin board.

The first official **Thanksgiving Festival Planning Committee Meeting** had the vibe of a sitcom episode and the energy of a caffeine-fueled PTA brawl. Claire had arrived early — sugar cookies in a festive tin, pumpkin earrings swinging with every step — and placed them neatly in the center of the conference table.

Eli arrived exactly on time, looked at the cookies, looked at her, and said, "What is that, bribery?"

Claire smiled sweetly. "No. Charm. It's called charm. You should try it sometime."

He didn't answer, but took a cookie anyway.

FIFTEEN MINUTES LATER, **chaos reigned.**

The room was packed with local business owners, volunteers,

and a suspiciously large group of retired ladies from the quilting club who all had clipboards and strong opinions.

Eli tried to take charge like he was running a Michelin-starred kitchen.

"We'll need three prep stations, a sanitation zone, and no one is roasting anything that hasn't been inspected by—"

"I'm not giving up my stuffing recipe," shouted Mr. Dunlop, who ran the hardware store and apparently considered Stove Top a sacred tradition.

"Stuffing is fine," countered Mrs. Beasley from the pie shop, "but mashed potatoes are what people actually *eat*."

"I *eat* stuffing!" yelled someone from the back.

Claire sat in the middle of it, eyes wide, sipping cider like she was watching a reality show unfold.

And then—suddenly, like lightning striking a butterball—she stood.

"Alright, alright, alright!" she called over the din. "Clearly, this is important. So let's *make* it important."

Everyone turned.

Claire held up her cookie tin like it was a gavel.

"We settle this the old-fashioned way: a **Stuffing vs. Mashed Potato Showdown**. Two tables. Two teams. One crown. The people vote with their forks."

A beat of silence.

Eli, arms folded, stared at her. "Are you serious?"

Claire grinned. "Always."

He didn't smile. But something in his eyes flickered — a tiny, grudging spark of respect.

"Fine," he said. "But I'm not dressing up like a side dish mascot."

THE MEETING FINALLY ENDED.

The retirees filed out whispering conspiratorially. Eli lingered, gathering his notes. Claire, ever the multitasker, had rolled out her massive spiral-bound planner and was adding sticky tabs in pumpkin and cranberry colors.

"You're really doing all that for a food festival?" Eli asked, watching her scribble in multiple pens.

Claire looked up, caught off-guard. "Of course. People plan weddings with less emotion than they feel about green bean casserole. Plus... I like making things feel special. Organized chaos, but with glitter."

Eli leaned over the table to glance at her calendar, and for a moment, they were close — too close. Claire caught a whiff of something warm and woodsy, and forgot the day of the week.

Then she saw *his* notes.

He had sketched the entire barn layout by hand — perfectly proportioned, shaded, labeled, with a separate diagram for the cider station plumbing setup. It looked like something out of a high-end kitchen design catalog.

She stared, genuinely impressed.

"This is... really good."

He shrugged. "You have your pens. I have blueprints."

Claire smiled. "This man is intense," she thought. "But kind of a genius."

THEN IT HAPPENED — the kind of moment you don't plan, but remember anyway.

They both reached for the same notepad.

Fingers brushed.

Claire's hand pulled back like she'd touched a live wire.

Eli didn't move at all.

Their eyes met. Just for a second. Just long enough.

Then Claire cleared her throat. "Anyway."

"Yep," Eli said, stepping back. "Anyway."

. . .

Claire closed her planner, the edges lined with color and possibility.

"You might actually be fun when you're not grumbling," she said, voice light but not teasing.

Eli looked at her, the barest smile tugging at his lips. "Don't get used to it."

Outside the window, the sky was softening into twilight, the first hint of stars winking through the branches. Inside, something small and quiet had shifted.

Maybe it wasn't a war after all.

Maybe it was a dance.

CHAPTER 5
KITCHEN FIRES AND FLASHBACKS

S ome kitchens are built for warmth. Others are built for war. This one, on a Tuesday afternoon in late November, felt like both.

The **Harvest Hollow Community Center Kitchen** had exactly two functioning ovens, one flickering overhead light, and a smell of bleach that never quite left the tile. Claire Monroe stood at the prep station in a cranberry sweater, sleeves rolled up, cheeks dusted in flour and optimism.

Eli Hunter stood across from her, wielding a chef's knife like it owed him money.

"You're slicing too fast," he said.

Claire paused. "I'm literally slicing a pear."

"You're bruising it."

She looked at him. "You're bruising *me*."

He didn't smile. But the corner of his mouth almost twitched. Almost.

It had been **a long afternoon of recipe testing.**

Tension had simmered like soup left too long on the back burner.

Claire was trying to perfect her **maple butternut squash tartlets**, and Eli was prepping a **rosemary sage stuffing** that smelled like it had been kissed by the gods themselves. They were too close in the cramped space, constantly reaching for the same spatula, constantly biting back opinions. It was a kind of dance — sharp, hot, fast-paced.

And it was wearing them down.

Claire dropped her piping bag for the fifth time and groaned. "This kitchen is a crime against ergonomics."

Eli didn't look up. "It's functional."

"You'd say that about a shoebox if it had a sink."

"Only if it had counter space."

Claire bit her tongue, turned toward the stove, and didn't notice that the back burner — the one she'd tested cider on earlier — hadn't been turned off.

THE FIRE STARTED SMALL. **But it was still fire.**

There was a pop. Then a hiss. Then flame.

Claire screamed.

Eli moved fast — a blur of flannel and instinct — and grabbed the fire extinguisher from under the sink. A blast of white foam filled the air. The tartlets died a heroic death.

And then, silence.

Claire stood shaking, still clutching the handle of a pot she hadn't used in fifteen minutes.

Eli turned to her. "Are you okay?"

"I—yes—I think—I don't—" She blinked, heart racing. "I didn't even realize—"

"Clearly," he snapped.

And just like that, the anger landed.

"I was trying to—" she started.

"You were *distracted*. This isn't a tea party, Claire, it's a working kitchen!"

She flinched. His voice echoed. Harsh. Loud. Too much.

A beat passed. Two. Then Eli exhaled like he was trying to get the fire out of his *own* chest.

"Sorry," he said, quieter now. "I shouldn't've yelled."

Claire looked at him, unsure what to say.

He leaned back against the counter, rubbing a hand over his face, voice lower now. Rough. Real.

"This was supposed to be easy," he murmured. "A simple favor for the town. Not... not this."

Claire watched him. Something shifted in his shoulders — not anger. Weariness. Regret.

"What happened?" she asked softly.

He didn't look at her. Just stared at the foam-covered floor like it might answer for him.

"I used to run a restaurant," he said. "In New York. Ember & Ash. We had a Michelin star."

Claire's breath caught. She knew that name.

"That was *you*?" she whispered.

He nodded once. "Until it wasn't. Place burned down. Figuratively. Almost literally. Scandal, betrayal, headlines... you name it."

Claire moved a little closer, careful not to crowd him. "I remember reading something. There was a... sous-chef?"

His jaw tensed.

"She was more than that," he said, voice a little cracked around the edges. "We opened it together. And she closed it without telling me. One bad night. One worse decision. The whole thing collapsed."

Claire swallowed. She saw it now — the guarded glances, the way he held everything just out of reach. His silence wasn't arrogance. It was armor.

"I'm sorry," she said.

He nodded, staring at the wall. "I haven't cooked in front of people since."

"You're cooking now."

"It's different."

"No," Claire said, voice steady, "it's brave."

The silence between them softened.

The kitchen was still a mess. Tartlets ruined. Air sharp with extinguisher dust.

But Claire didn't care about that.

"You know," she said gently, "people mess up. It doesn't mean you stop cooking."

Eli didn't look at her, not right away. When he did, there was something raw in his expression. Honest.

"Sometimes it does," he said.

They stood in that quiet together, not fixing anything. Not pretending to.

Just... standing.

Claire gathered her things slowly, pausing by the door before she left.

She turned back, eyes softer now, voice low. "We've got five days, Chef Hunter. Let's not burn the place down before the stuffing gets made."

Eli looked up from the wreckage of their shared chaos, something unreadable in his gaze.

Then he nodded, once.

And for the first time since they met, Claire felt like maybe he'd let her in — even if just by a crack.

CHAPTER 6
THE GREAT PIE-OFF

It was the kind of Saturday that tasted like cinnamon and felt like the beginning of something good. The sun had risen with a golden yawn over Maple Acres Barn, casting soft light on hay bales dressed in gingham and picnic tables dusted with powdered sugar. Kids with frosting on their cheeks darted between pumpkin stacks, and someone in the distance played a banjo version of "American Pie" like it was a sacred hymn.

Claire Monroe stood at the entrance of the barn, clipboard in one hand and a paper coffee cup in the other, taking it all in with a chestful of cautious pride. The **Great Pie-Off**, her brainchild and personal masterpiece of organized chaos, had officially begun. Local bakers from across Harvest Hollow had shown up with flaky pride and homemade aprons, their pies ranging from "Grandma's Secret Apple" to "Experimental Vegan Pudding That May or May Not Be Legal."

There were too many pies. Not enough napkins. The whipped cream station had already collapsed once.

It was perfect.

And sitting beside her, armed with a tasting fork and an expression of weary judgment, was none other than Chef Eli Hunter — Harvest Hollow's official pie skeptic.

"You know," he said as he surveyed the first entry — a neon pink strawberry cream thing that wobbled suspiciously in its foil — "this feels more like a sugar ambush than a festival."

Claire leaned closer, whispering theatrically, "Be brave. The people need your palate."

Eli raised an eyebrow. "This isn't pie. It's a crime against butter."

Claire snorted. "Says the man who thinks whipped cream should be 'complex.'"

"It *should* be. It's cream. With ambition."

By the third slice, they were both halfway to a sugar coma, but the banter had found a rhythm, and so had they. Locals gathered not just to see who would win the golden rolling pin trophy, but to watch them — the grump and the sunshine — spar their way through caramel drizzles and questionable crusts.

"That's not a crust," Eli murmured at one point, frowning into a cherry slab. "That's a structural tragedy."

Claire grinned, nudging him. "Careful, someone might think you're enjoying yourself."

He looked at her — and then, without meaning to, without guarding it — he laughed. Really laughed. Deep and low and startlingly warm.

Claire blinked. For a moment, her brain stopped cataloging the pies and just... noticed him. There was something different about Eli when he laughed. Something unguarded. Unpracticed. His features softened, and the tension that usually coiled tight around his shoulders unraveled like ribbon.

Less storm cloud, more smolder, she thought suddenly, and then wanted to throw herself into the whipped cream bucket for thinking it.

The rest of the afternoon blurred into a whirl of votes and applause. Little kids handed them slices with sticky fingers and hopeful eyes. Someone brought a bourbon pecan pie that nearly made Claire cry. Eli actually complimented a crust. The town buzzed with the kind of joy that came from being a little full, a little silly, and a little in love with life.

That night, back at her cottage, Claire curled up on the couch in leggings and fuzzy socks, laptop balanced on her knees, and edited the footage she'd collected throughout the day. Eli frowning into a pie. Eli's eyes widening in cautious delight. Eli laughing, just once, the kind of laugh that made you want to hear it again.

She added soft indie music in the background. Warm autumn tones. Text overlay that read:

"Grumpiest chef in town. Secretly a pie whisperer. #PumpkinSpiceKisses #HarvestHollow"

She posted it without thinking too hard. Then she curled deeper into her blanket, heart doing that annoying little flutter thing.

THE NEXT MORNING, her phone buzzed just after sunrise.

Eli Hunter: *You caught my good side. Don't get used to it.*

Claire stared at the message, cheeks blooming pink in the soft light of dawn. She typed, erased, then typed again.

Claire Monroe: *Too late.*

CHAPTER 7
WHISKED AWAY

Some days don't start with sparks — they begin with something missing.

In this case, it was **honeycrisp apples**, which might not seem catastrophic to the untrained eye, but to Claire Monroe — who was mid-demo for her caramel apple crumble cups and two days away from the live "Taste of Thanksgiving" showcase — it was enough to induce a mild spiral.

The box from the supplier had been mislabeled, and instead of crisp, tart beauties that snapped when bitten, Claire was left with bruised golden delicious and one very offended expression. "This is sabotage," she muttered, holding up an apple like a piece of evidence. "They knew."

Eli, who had been quietly chopping herbs and ignoring her melodrama, finally looked up. "There's a farmer two towns over. If we leave now, we'll make it back before setup."

Claire blinked. "Wait, *we?*"

He sighed. "You'll get lost."

"I will not—" she started, then saw his expression. He wasn't offering. He was *already grabbing his jacket.*

THANKFUL HEARTS AND PUMPKIN SPICE KISSES

. . .

The drive was longer than necessary but filled with everything Claire secretly loved: winding roads dressed in orange and gold, thermoses of cider balanced in cupholders, and a playlist that somehow went from Brandi Carlile to classic Beatles without missing a beat. Eli sat in the passenger seat, staring out at the passing trees, while Claire stole glances at him — half curious, half mesmerized.

They didn't talk much at first. The silence between them wasn't awkward, just… cautious. Like neither of them wanted to ruin whatever strange, tentative thread had been tying them together lately.

Then Claire offered him a piece of her pumpkin spice granola bar and said, "No judgment if you hate it."

He bit into it, chewed, then shrugged. "Needs salt."

Claire grinned. "You're consistent, I'll give you that."

"Flavored cardboard is still cardboard."

"You're lucky you're pretty."

He blinked at her, startled.

She kept her eyes on the road and smiled.

They reached the orchard just as the late afternoon sun dipped behind the hills, and Claire made an embarrassingly enthusiastic sound when she spotted the hand-painted *"Fresh Apples & Warm Cider"* sign swinging in the breeze. Eli watched her with an expression that might have been amusement, or fondness, or something softer still.

On the drive back, with two crates of apples in the backseat and the scent of cinnamon clinging to her sweater, Claire suggested they stop at the little roadside diner glowing at the edge of town. "I've passed it three times this week," she said. "It has fairy lights. That's a sign from the universe."

Eli hesitated, then nodded. "Fine. But I'm not eating anything labeled 'world-famous' if it was made in a microwave."

THE DINER WAS the kind of place where the booths were cracked and the jukebox only played three songs, but the pie was warm and the air smelled like stories. Claire ordered apple pie — because of course she did — and Eli didn't argue when she ordered one for him, too.

They talked. About little things at first. Favorite kitchen disasters. Her deep and abiding fear of soufflés. His irrational dislike of decorative gourds.

Then, somewhere between bites of pie and the last flicker of sunlight across their table, the stories deepened.

Claire told him about growing up with holidays that never quite landed right. How her mom tried too hard and her dad didn't try at all. How Thanksgiving always felt like the one time the chaos paused — where a meal could hold everything together, even if just for an hour.

Eli listened. Really listened. Then, after a pause, he said, "I built Ember & Ash to be more than a restaurant. It was supposed to be a place where my team could belong. Safe. Solid. Like family."

Claire didn't speak. Just watched him.

He didn't look at her, but his fingers tapped gently against the table. "When it all collapsed, I didn't just lose my name or reputation. I lost *them*. And I... I didn't know how to rebuild after that."

The pie sat half-eaten between them.

Claire reached out, almost without thinking, and brushed her hand over his. Just once.

"It still matters," she said quietly. "What you built. Even if it didn't last."

Eli looked up at her then — fully — and she saw it in his eyes. The rawness. The regret. And beneath all of it, a glimmer of hope that scared him more than anything else.

. . .

Later, under the stars outside the diner, the world felt smaller and softer somehow. They stood beside Claire's car, the silence stretching between them again — but different now. Familiar. Safe.

She looked up at him, smile gone tender.

He looked back, gaze intense and searching.

Claire tilted her head just slightly. A signal.

Eli leaned in. Just enough. Just slowly enough that it didn't feel like a kiss — it felt like a question.

And then her phone rang.

A sharp, digital sound slicing through the moment like a dropped plate.

Claire blinked, pulled back, and fumbled for her phone.

Logan, the name read. Her ex. Her former co-host. The one who always called when things were going too well.

Eli stepped back, just once. Not angry. Just… guarded again.

Claire silenced the call.

But the moment was gone.

She looked at him, apology blooming in her eyes. "Sorry. It's—work."

Eli gave her a small nod, but his voice was quiet again, the wall sliding back into place.

"We should get going."

CHAPTER 8
PAST ITS EXPIRATION DATE

Some truths don't arrive with fireworks. They slip in through the side door, carried by the smell of old coffee and the kind of silence that knows too much.

It was early. The barn kitchen smelled like cinnamon and wet wood, and the light pouring through the windows was soft, almost reluctant, as if even the sun knew that something delicate was about to be said.

Claire sat on the worn stool by the long prep table, fingers curled around a chipped mug of chai. Across from her, Eli leaned against the counter, arms folded tight like they were the only thing keeping him from unraveling.

"I figured you should hear it from me," he said, voice low. "Before someone else twists it."

Claire didn't interrupt. Just nodded once.

Eli exhaled. Long. Heavy. And then he told her.

About **Ember & Ash**. The dream he built from the ground up with a woman he trusted. A woman he loved. About the way everything began to fracture — a missed reservation here, a cold dish there, and then one night, when a food critic walked through the door and everything went sideways. And how, afterward, when the bad review hit, it wasn't just disappointment waiting — it was betrayal.

"She leaked the emails," he said. "Private ones. From our investors. From me. Things taken out of context and twisted into scandal. Headlines exploded overnight."

Claire stared at him, chest tight.

"She said she did it to protect us," Eli added, a bitter laugh catching in his throat. "But she'd already signed a solo deal by then."

Silence stretched between them. Not empty, but loaded.

Claire wanted to say something — anything — but what words were there for betrayal that deep?

"I haven't cooked in front of a crowd since," he said. "Haven't let anyone in, really. Until now."

Claire blinked, her vision going soft around the edges.

"I'm not her," she said quietly.

"I know," he replied.

But his voice wasn't so sure.

Later that afternoon, Claire sat alone on a hay bale outside the barn, her phone buzzing in her lap. The message she'd been pretending not to expect had finally arrived.

Subject: L.A. Holiday Pilot — Claire Monroe?

A network executive. One she admired. One who, apparently, had seen the pie reel she'd posted a few days ago — the one with Eli laughing, the one she edited with more care than she'd like to admit.

They wanted her to fly out *right after the festival*. Screen-test. Film a pilot. Potentially launch her own holiday cooking show.

It was everything she had worked for.

Everything she'd dreamed of.

So why did her stomach twist?

She read the email three times. Typed a reply. Deleted it. Set her phone down, picked it up again. Her fingers trembled, just slightly.

. . .

By evening, the barn was buzzing with activity. Volunteers strung paper lanterns between rafters while tables were draped in autumn cloths. There was laughter. Music. The hum of something about to come alive.

Claire stood at the far end of the barn, brushing her fingers over the edge of a serving tray, but her mind was elsewhere. She hadn't told Eli. Not yet.

She looked up — and there he was, across the barn, adjusting a ladder for one of the teens helping hang lanterns. He looked at her. Smiled. She tried to return it, but it faltered halfway through.

He noticed.

Of course he did.

Later, when they stood side by side reviewing the event timeline, Eli glanced at her out of the corner of his eye.

"You're quiet today," he said.

Claire shrugged. "Just tired."

But they both knew it was a lie.

That night, the air was cool and the lanterns glowed like tiny suns above them. The barn felt like a dream just before waking — warm, too good to be true, too fragile to last.

Claire leaned against the wooden frame of the open barn door, arms wrapped around herself. She watched the glow spill out onto the grass, painting the dark with flickers of hope.

Eli joined her, quietly.

They didn't speak for a while.

And then, softly, Claire asked, "What if we don't get another shot at something like this?"

The question hung between them like a breath that hadn't decided whether to fall or fly.

Eli looked at her, then at the lights, then at the stars beyond.

"Then," he said, voice barely more than a whisper, "we make the most of it while we have it."

Claire didn't say anything. But she stayed standing next to him a little longer than she needed to.

Because maybe staying — just for a while — was enough.

CHAPTER 9
CORNBREAD & CONFESSIONS

S ome nights feel borrowed from a better world — sweeter, slower, like the universe is letting you hold its hand for just a little while.

The barn was quiet except for the occasional creak of wood and the low hum of fairy lights warming to life along the rafters. It was the night before the big "Taste & Tour" showcase, and Claire and Eli had stayed late to prep the final touches — folding table linens, lighting candles, and slicing endless trays of cornbread, which filled the space with the kind of scent that made you want to write home or fall in love. Maybe both.

Claire was kneeling beside a box of lanterns when an old folk song began playing from the portable speaker near Eli's station. It was soft, the kind of song that sounded like rocking chairs and rainy porches. She looked up.

Eli stood a few feet away, wiping his hands on a towel, the music catching him mid-step. For a moment, their eyes met in the golden glow. It was a quiet kind of invitation.

"Dance with me," Claire said, surprising even herself.

Eli's eyebrows lifted. "I don't dance."

"Liar," she replied, standing. "You're just afraid I'll outshine you."

He shook his head but didn't say no. After a pause, he stepped closer and offered his hand — a little stiff, a little hesitant — but warm. Claire placed hers in his, and they moved into the space between hay bales and prep tables, just the two of them and the hush of a barn full of light.

At first, it was awkward. She stepped on his foot. He muttered something about rhythm being overrated. But then — somehow — they found it. The rhythm. The ease. The quiet.

Claire leaned into his chest, cheek brushing flannel. She could hear his heartbeat, steady and solid. Eli's hand slid gently to the small of her back, his other still clasping hers. He tilted his head just slightly, and their eyes met again — this time slower, softer, as if seeing each other for the first time in a way that truly counted.

And then he tilted her chin.

And then he kissed her.

Sweet. Tender. Like he meant it. Like he wasn't used to meaning things but had decided, just this once, to try.

Claire melted into him, hands curled in his shirt, the world narrowing to this one golden moment where everything made sense.

Until it didn't.

THE SOUND OF FOOTSTEPS. A clearing throat.

"Hope you're not mixing business and pleasure again, Eli," came a voice from the shadows.

They broke apart like teenagers caught under the bleachers.

Mayor Langford stood near the doorway, clipboard in hand, trying to look casual and failing miserably.

Eli's jaw tightened. Claire blinked, confused.

Again?

The mayor gave a stiff nod and left, but the words stayed, hanging in the air like smoke from a snuffed candle.

· · ·

Later, Claire found Eli alone, cleaning up the last of the cornbread trays. The warmth from before had vanished. He was quiet again. Guarded.

She stepped closer. "What did he mean, 'again'?"

Eli didn't look at her right away. Then, without emotion, he said, "My ex. The sous-chef I told you about."

Claire's breath caught.

"She wasn't just a partner in the kitchen," he continued. "She was also... invested. Financially. Publicly. We built Ember & Ash together. People assumed we were a power couple." He laughed bitterly. "Turns out we were just an implosion waiting to happen."

Claire felt her pulse stutter. "So it wasn't just betrayal. It was... all of it."

He nodded. "She sold her shares. Told the press I'd sidelined her. Made herself the victim. And I was too angry to defend myself the right way. So the story stuck."

Claire's mouth went dry. This wasn't just messy. This was *his entire reputation*. And here she was, halfway through falling for him, tied to him by a project that might blow up in both their faces if things went wrong.

And now L.A. was waiting. A call she hadn't returned. An opportunity that would take her across the country and leave behind something fragile and new and already so complicated.

Was she about to be part of another "bad ending" in his story?

Was he going to be one in hers?

She stepped back. Just a little. Enough that he noticed.

"I just... I need to think," she whispered.

He didn't stop her.

Didn't say a word.

Just watched her go, eyes shadowed and still, like he'd seen this scene before and already knew how it would end.

. . .

Claire walked out into the cool night, her breath curling in front of her like smoke.

Behind her, the barn lights glowed soft and gold, like they were still trying to hold onto the warmth they'd made together.

But some things, she was beginning to realize, didn't stay warm forever.

CHAPTER 10
THE FALLOUT

Sometimes, the worst storms don't come from the sky. They build slowly inside people — behind narrowed eyes and tight-lipped smiles — and by the time they break, the damage is already done.

The morning after the kiss — after the mayor's comment, after the truth — Claire showed up to the barn with a forced smile and a tin of cranberry-orange muffins she didn't remember baking. She greeted the volunteers, laughed a little too loudly, adjusted table linens that didn't need adjusting.

Eli didn't look at her.

He moved like a shadow behind her — quiet, sharp, all business. No trace of the man who had kissed her like she was something he'd waited for. His voice, when he spoke to her, was clipped. Cordial. Not unkind — but miles away from the softness she'd felt pressed against her in the dark.

Claire tried to pretend it didn't hurt. But it did. It ached like a bruise under every breath.

She knew what this was. Knew how it felt when someone started pulling away before they said the words. And somehow, that hurt more than anything else — because for once, she had actually believed in the possibility of something different.

The sky began to change by late afternoon.

Dark clouds rolled over the hills like a warning. Wind crept in through the barn doors, rattling the lantern strings they'd spent hours perfecting. Eli paused his prep to glance outside, brows drawn.

"Forecast said clear," Claire said, trying for casual.

Eli didn't answer.

By evening, the storm was no longer a suggestion — it was a promise. Thunder cracked like a warning shot, and then came the rain. Not gentle. Not poetic. Furious sheets that slammed the windows and soaked the ground within minutes.

Claire stood at the barn entrance, heart sinking.

The tents were the first to go — one ripped free and tumbled down the hill like a ghostly kite. The welcome banner tore in half, fluttering uselessly in the wind. Lights flickered. Water pooled around the prep tables outside.

It wasn't just a storm.

It was ruin.

And it felt eerily familiar.

By the time they'd managed to get most of the food and supplies indoors, the walkways were flooded and the farm grounds looked like a washed-out painting. Everyone was soaked. Mud streaked the floor. Spirits were sinking faster than the thermometer.

The festival — their festival — was falling apart.

And Claire, who had held it together all day, finally cracked.

She turned to Eli, rain in her eyes, voice trembling. "This was supposed to be *good*, Eli. For the town. For us. For *once*, it felt like something might actually go *right*."

He looked at her — but didn't step closer. Didn't say anything.

Claire took a breath that shook. "Why does everything always break right when it's getting better?"

Silence.

Eli opened his mouth.

Then closed it again.

Claire's heart twisted. "Say something. *Anything*."

But he didn't.

He just stood there, jaw tight, fists clenched at his sides like he was holding back a thousand things — and had decided to say none of them.

So Claire turned.

She walked away.

Out into the storm, into the wind and mud and heartbreak, until the barn lights blurred behind her in the rain.

She didn't look back.

But Eli did.

He stood in the barn doorway, soaked and silent, and watched her disappear — fists still clenched, words still unspoken, heart still too afraid to follow.

The thunder cracked overhead.

And in the space it left behind, something else broke quietly — something they'd both been too scared to name.

CHAPTER 11
FRIENDSGIVING FAIL?

Some things are worth saving — not because they went perfectly, but because someone chose to fight for them anyway.

Claire Monroe stood at the front of the dim, damp barn, surrounded by scattered chairs, wilting centerpieces, and the unmistakable smell of rain-soaked regret. Everything was broken. Not just the decorations or the downed lanterns or the water-logged entry signs — *everything*. Her confidence. Her connection with Eli. The fragile little world they had built together, one pie and eye roll at a time.

She looked around at the tired faces of the volunteers, their jackets damp and boots caked in mud. No one said it out loud, but they all thought it: *The festival's over.*

Claire cleared her throat.

"Okay," she said, trying to keep her voice from shaking, "what if we move it?"

Heads turned.

"To where?" someone asked. "The moon?"

Claire pointed toward the window, toward the heart of town. "Main Street. We hang the lights from the lampposts. Line the sidewalks with hay bales. Food booths in front of the storefronts. Lanterns overhead. We call it a pop-up Thanksgiving stroll. Cozy. Casual. A little chaotic, but magical."

Silence.

Then Lucy, her best friend and unofficial emotional bodyguard, nodded slowly. "It could work."

"But it'd have to be done *fast*," said someone from the back.

Claire took a deep breath. "We don't need to rebuild the whole barn. We just need enough. Enough warmth. Enough food. Enough heart. That's what people remember anyway."

There was a long pause.

And then, from the back of the room, a voice said, "One last Hail Mary, huh?"

It was Eli.

He stepped forward, hands in his jacket pockets, hair still damp from the storm, eyes unreadable — but not closed off. Not this time.

Claire met his gaze. "One last."

He held it for a beat.

Then he nodded.

The next twelve hours were a blur of lists and ladders and last-minute miracles. People trickled in, one by one — Lucy's cousin brought extra tents, the bakery down the street donated day-old pastries, the high school theater club offered to hang lanterns and string lights in exchange for cider and credit.

Still, the energy was low. Spirits sagged under the weight of too much water and not enough sleep.

Until Eli spoke.

He stood in the center of Main Street, a coil of lights in one hand, and raised his voice just enough to carry.

"Look, I know this wasn't the plan. I know it's not going to be polished. Or perfect. But Thanksgiving was never about that. It's about showing up. Being together. Even if the stuffing is cold and the table's crooked."

People paused, looked up.

Eli cleared his throat. "I've messed up before. Big. And I spent a lot of time thinking that if I couldn't do it perfectly, I shouldn't do it at all. But I was wrong. What matters is that we're *here*. That we try. That we make something out of the mess."

And just like that, something shifted.

People started moving faster, laughing louder. Someone plugged in a speaker and started playing music. Lanterns rose again like sleepy stars coming back to life.

Claire watched Eli from a distance, a coil tightening and loosening in her chest all at once.

He hadn't just stepped up.

He'd *opened up*.

And it cracked something in her wide open, too.

Because suddenly, it wasn't just about saving the festival or proving she could pull something off — it was about him. About the man who had been afraid to let people back in, who had kissed her like it mattered, who stood in the rain and *didn't stop her from leaving*, not because he didn't care, but because he didn't think he deserved to ask her to stay.

And still, here he was.

Helping. Healing. Showing up.

That was love, wasn't it?

Not the fairytale, but the choosing. The showing up.

As the first lanterns were strung across the lampposts, glowing softly against the twilight sky, Claire leaned against Lucy's shoulder, heart pounding in a quiet, sure way.

"This town," she whispered. "This man."

Lucy arched a brow, smirking.

"I wasn't planning on falling," Claire murmured. "But I think I did."

CHAPTER 12
THE NIGHT BEFORE

Some nights wrap themselves around you like a secret — quiet, golden, a little fragile — as if the world has paused just long enough for you to feel everything you were trying not to.

The town of Harvest Hollow was asleep, tucked beneath a navy sky strewn with stars. The streets, lit by faint string lights, were still damp from the storm. Shop windows reflected soft glows and unfinished decorations, and somewhere, a wind chime whispered like a lullaby on the breeze.

But behind the back door of **Eli's restaurant**, in a makeshift prep kitchen cobbled together with folding tables, electric burners, and hope, two people were very much awake.

Claire Monroe rolled dough with flour-dusted elbows, her hair pulled into a high, messy bun that had surrendered hours ago. Across from her, Eli worked with methodical grace, brow furrowed in thought as he lined trays with parchment. They moved in a rhythm now — no tripping over each other, no biting remarks — just the soft shuffle of feet, the clink of metal, and the quiet harmony of people who had learned how to share a space.

Neither spoke much.

They didn't have to.

The silence was easy. Warm. It said: *You're safe here.*

It was nearly midnight, and exhaustion should have made them clumsy, short-tempered. But instead, it made them soft. Claire had stopped trying to impress him. Eli had stopped trying to intimidate her. And in the space between those things, something honest had grown.

Claire slid another tray of mini pies onto the counter, biting her lip when she noticed the slightly burnt edges. "Ugh. I ruined this batch."

Eli stepped over, took one look, and gently reached for the tray. "No, you didn't."

He carefully trimmed the edge of one, flicking the golden crust away with the precision of a surgeon and the patience of a teacher. Claire watched him work, eyes lingering on the way his hands moved — strong, sure, kind.

He looked up just as she was looking down.

Then reached out and brushed a smudge of flour from her cheek.

His thumb lingered a second longer than it should have. Neither of them breathed.

When he finally pulled away, Claire felt something shift in her chest. Not fireworks. Not chaos. Something simpler. Softer. Like a door creaking open inside her that she wasn't sure she wanted to close.

LATER, when the prep was done, when the pies were lined in perfect rows and the last spoon had been licked clean of pumpkin batter, Claire leaned against the counter with a sigh. Her shoulders sagged. Her feet ached. And her heart was heavier than it had been just hours before.

She hadn't told him.

About the email.

About L.A.

The opportunity still sat in her inbox, shining like a spotlight: *"Flight confirmed. See you Monday."*

It was everything she'd worked for.

But when she looked at Eli — sleeves rolled up, hands dusted in flour, that quiet focus in his eyes — she didn't know how to say, *I might be leaving.*

And Eli... he didn't ask. But he looked at her like he already knew.

He glanced over once as she rubbed her eyes, and in his expression, she saw it — the question he wanted to ask, the fear behind it.

Stay.

But the word never came.

He didn't want to ask her to give up her dream.

And Claire didn't want to break this quiet spell with the weight of reality.

So they said nothing.

Just shared the silence.

CLAIRE CURLED up on the small couch in the corner of the kitchen, knees tucked beneath her, a blanket wrapped around her shoulders. Eli moved around quietly, turning off burners, stacking dishes, wiping down counters.

He paused as he passed her — hesitant, ready to say goodnight — and that's when she reached out.

She caught his hand.

"I don't want to be alone tonight," she said, voice barely above a whisper.

He didn't speak.

Just nodded.

Then sat down beside her.

. . .

THEY DIDN'T KISS.

They didn't need to.

Instead, they lay tangled on the couch like a page from a story left open in the middle of a sentence — her head against his shoulder, his arm around her waist, their legs tangled and warm beneath the old knit blanket.

It wasn't passionate.

It was real.

It was the kind of closeness that meant more than anything they hadn't yet said aloud.

Claire stayed awake for a while, staring at the shadows flickering across the wall, listening to the even sound of his breathing.

This wasn't in the plan, she thought. *But neither was he. And suddenly, I don't know what the plan even is anymore.*

She closed her eyes.

And for the first time in a long time, she didn't feel like she had to keep moving to matter.

CHAPTER END HOOK:

The sun hadn't risen yet, but the sky was beginning to lighten — a soft blue bruising the edges of the night. Morning crept in gently, through the cracks in the windowpanes, spilling over the counter, the flour-dusted floors, and the small couch where they slept.

Claire stirred first.

She blinked in the glow of early light and smiled when she saw Eli still asleep beside her, his hand resting in hers, his face calm in a way she rarely saw.

And then, her phone buzzed.

A single vibration on the edge of the table.

She reached for it with sleep-heavy fingers.

Flight confirmed. See you Monday in L.A. — bring your A-game.

Claire's smile faded.

She looked down at Eli, still curled beside her.

And for the first time, she felt the weight of *leaving* more than the thrill of *going*.

CHAPTER 13
MAIN STREET MAGIC

Sometimes, the most magical moments are the ones you never planned — the ones born from broken pieces and stitched together with hope, tape, and too many extension cords.

Main Street had never looked so beautiful.

Where there had once been puddles and mud now stood rows of string lights stretching across rooftops like stars had chosen to settle there. Bunting in deep fall hues waved gently in the breeze. Hay bales had been dressed in plaid blankets and tucked into every corner, as if the entire town had been wrapped in comfort. Shopkeepers stood proudly in their doorways, some holding warm mugs, others offering samples of cornbread or cider, and above it all stretched a hand-painted banner: **Taste of Thanksgiving**.

Claire Monroe stood in the center of it all, utterly still.

She wasn't holding a camera. Or a clipboard. Or a latte. Just her own breath, caught tight in her chest. Because it was *working*. The festival — the one that had been stormed out, burned down, and pieced back together with bare hands — had bloomed. It was messy. A little crooked. But completely, heart-wrenchingly beautiful.

She turned slowly, taking it all in. The flannel-wearing kids with caramel apples. The elderly quilting club running a jam tasting booth. The smell of roasted turkey mingling with cinnamon and woodsmoke. Music floated through the street, played by a local band who barely had their instruments tuned but made up for it in cheer.

And then there was **Eli.**

He stood near the pie stand in a simple button-down, sleeves rolled up, apron dusted in flour, surrounded by half a dozen eager tasters and not looking remotely as grumpy as he was pretending to be.

He caught her eye.

And smiled.

Just for her.

By mid-afternoon, the highlight of the day arrived: the **Stuffing vs. Mashed Potato Showdown.**

A crowd formed quickly — families in scarves, teenagers with cider, toddlers bouncing in knit hats. Claire stood on a crate in the middle of it all, arms raised like a carnival barker, voice ringing over the crowd.

"Ladies and gentlemen, prepare your taste buds and cast your loyalty! Will it be Team *Stuff It* or Team *Spud Squad* that takes home the golden gravy boat?"

The contestants wore matching t-shirts, Claire had made little candy corn "ballots" to place in two giant glass jars, and Eli — standing beside her with a wooden spoon tucked into his apron — looked vaguely like he wanted the ground to swallow him whole.

"This is humiliating," he muttered.

"This is *branding*," she grinned.

He mock-glared.

She nudged him with her elbow. "Smile. Just once. For the children."

He smiled. *For her.*

. . .

The crowd voted. With drama. With passionate speeches. With candy corn being thrown into jars like it was confetti. When the final vote was cast — a six-year-old girl in a tutu choosing mashed potatoes — Claire raised her hands in surrender.

"Spud Squad wins by *three kernels*!"

Eli raised a smug brow.

Claire bowed with mock regret. "I demand a recount."

The crowd roared with laughter, and as they dispersed, full of starch and satisfaction, Claire looked over at Eli — who was still watching her, an unreadable softness in his eyes.

They stood there for a heartbeat too long. His arm brushed hers. She didn't move away.

But just as Claire raised her mug of cider to toast their chaotic success, her phone buzzed.

Once. Twice.

She checked the screen.

It was her agent.

"The producer wants to do a live sit-down. Today. In thirty minutes. You in?"

Claire's fingers hovered over the screen, cider forgotten. She didn't move.

Then she looked at Eli.

"Hey," she said softly, pulling him aside, away from the crowd, into the little alley behind the bakery where no one was watching. "I just got a call. A network exec. They want a quick interview. Like… now."

Eli's jaw tensed just slightly. "You're leaving?"

"Just for a bit," she said, too quickly. "I'll be back in an hour. Two, tops."

He nodded.

But she saw the flicker behind his eyes. The one that said *You're not coming back.*

"You're going to be great," he said, quietly. No sarcasm. No teasing. Just... resigned encouragement. Like someone who didn't know how to say *please stay* without sounding selfish.

Claire hesitated.

She wanted to say something — something real. But nothing came out.

So she just touched his arm and whispered, "Save me a seat."

He didn't answer.

And that silence said everything.

She walked away in heels too fast for cobblestones, weaving between booths and lanterns and families gathered at folding tables.

When she reached the edge of Main Street, she paused.

Turned back.

Looked for him.

Eli was still there, standing in the same spot, arms crossed, watching the crowd but not really seeing it.

He didn't wave.

Claire turned away and kept walking.

The air was colder now. Or maybe she just felt it more.

Because some goodbyes don't come with closure. They come with cider in your hand, hope in your heart, and someone standing still behind you — waiting, but no longer asking.

CHAPTER 14
PUMPKIN SPICE KISSES

There are moments when time pauses—not because of silence, but because of *knowing*. Not because the world stops, but because your heart does. Claire Monroe sat under the warm buzz of studio lights with a camera lens trained on her and a voice in her ear reminding her to smile. The set of the local affiliate station was dressed with fake pumpkins, a small table full of prop pies, and a backdrop painted to look like the town she'd just run through and left behind. Her curls had been touched up, her sweater steamed, her eyeliner reapplied—but none of that could erase the storm still swirling in her chest. She'd left the festival at its peak. Left Eli standing there, not asking her to stay but not stopping her from going either. And now she was here, pretending to be steady.

The interviewer smiled brightly, cue cards in hand. "So, Claire, tell us—what's been the most rewarding part of organizing this event? Especially given how last-minute it all was?"

Claire opened her mouth, ready to launch into a practiced line about community, about creative solutions, about small-town grit. But the words stuck. Her throat tightened. And for the first time in years, she spoke without a script.

"It reminded me," she said slowly, voice wobbling just a little, "that food isn't just about flavor. Or technique. Or presentation. It's about connection. About how we take care of each other. And someone... someone reminded me of that when I'd forgotten it." She didn't say his name, but she didn't need to. It was written all over her face, every line of it soft with something unspoken but very, very real.

Back in the square, under golden light and the last traces of sunset, the festival crowd had gathered to watch the broadcast on a projector hastily mounted against the side of the bakery. Children leaned against their parents. Cider was sipped. Hands were held. And standing near the back, silent and still, was Eli. His apron was gone, replaced by his oldest flannel. There was flour on his jeans, but he hadn't noticed.

He stared at the screen like it was a window into a life he hadn't believed he deserved until now. Watching Claire speak—her eyes shining, her voice full of truth—he felt something in him break open. And it wasn't fear this time. It was clarity. Love, deep and terrifying, swelled in his chest like a second heartbeat. Not the kind that asks politely. The kind that *insists*.

Lucy stood beside him, arms crossed, watching his face instead of the screen. When the interview cut to commercial, she bumped his arm with her elbow and said, "Well? What are you waiting for, Chef?"

He didn't answer. He didn't need to.

Claire had just pulled off her mic and thanked the crew when she glanced down at her phone and saw the time. The lantern ceremony. The one she'd promised herself she wouldn't miss. Without a word, she kicked off her heels, grabbed her coat, and ran.

The streets of Harvest Hollow blurred around her, lights stretching like streamers as she darted past shop windows and glowing jack-o'-lanterns. Her breath came fast, her scarf trailing behind her, her heart beating with something between urgency and hope. She turned the corner just as the first lanterns began to rise, glowing paper against a velvet sky, floating with the weight of gratitude and unspoken wishes.

The crowd was gathered in the square, eyes turned upward, mouths open in wonder. Claire pushed her way through just in time to see her lantern—**her** lantern—already lifting into the night, the message she'd scribbled onto it swirling faintly in the breeze: *Thank you for the second chance I never thought I'd want.*

And then she saw him.

Eli stood beneath the lights, holding a second lantern, untouched, in his hands. His eyes scanned the crowd, and when they found her—breathless, messy-haired, cheeks flushed from the cold and the running—he didn't look surprised.

"You made it," he said, voice low and a little awed.

Claire grinned, heart hammering. "Told you I was charming under pressure."

He looked down at the lantern in his hands. "I saved you one."

Together, without another word, they lit the tiny flame inside, watching it flicker to life and grow until it illuminated both their faces. She could feel the heat of his shoulder against hers. The weight of everything unspoken between them, suspended now in this quiet, glowing ritual.

They released the lantern into the night together, hands letting go in unison.

It floated upward slowly, spinning in the soft wind, joining the others already dotting the sky. Claire watched it rise, watched it disappear into the stars—and then turned to him.

"I'm not going anywhere," she whispered.

He didn't ask if she meant it. He didn't ask what changed.

He just kissed her.

Finally.

It wasn't the kind of kiss that sparked firecrackers or sent crowds into applause. It was the kind that slowed everything down. That said, *You're here. I'm here. And somehow, we made it through the mess.*

The crowd kept watching the sky, oblivious, as the kiss stretched long and steady under the lanterns. They stood in the center of Main Street—surrounded by cider stalls, leftover cornbread, and the magic of something real finally beginning.

And above them, golden lights kept rising.

CHAPTER 15
SECOND HELPINGS

Some mornings taste like endings. Others taste like beginnings wrapped in cinnamon steam and cider warmth, the kind that lingers on your tongue and makes you believe in the softness of the world all over again.

The morning after the festival smelled like hay, sugar, and tired joy. The sun climbed slowly over Harvest Hollow, gilding the empty food stalls and gently tousled bunting with sleepy gold. Claire Monroe walked beside Eli down the center of Main Street, the crunch of early frost beneath their boots, hot cider cupped between cold hands. Around them, the town stretched and yawned to life — volunteers wrapped cords, someone swept candy corn into a dustpan, and in the corner of the square, a group of children were playing tag between tipped-over hay bales like the whole world was their playground.

Claire watched them with a quiet smile. The laughter, the peace, the worn-out glow of a job well done — it all felt too good to be real. And maybe that was what made it even sweeter.

Eli glanced over at her, his hand brushing hers now and then, never lingering, but never far. They hadn't said much since the kiss. They hadn't needed to. The kiss had already said everything.

They sat on the courthouse steps, cider cups steaming in their laps, just watching the day unfold around them like the world had been turned one gentle degree closer to perfect.

"I told them no," Claire said, finally.

Eli turned. "The network?"

She nodded, her voice soft but certain. "I told them I wasn't leaving. That my story's here. My heart, too."

He didn't speak. But his eyes held hers, and in them, she saw it again — the thing she hadn't dared to name until now.

Love.

"They didn't hang up," she added with a laugh. "In fact, they offered to build a series around *Harvest Hollow*. A remote holiday cooking special. A whole show about the festival, the food… us. If we want it."

Eli blinked, slow and stunned. "Seriously?"

Claire grinned. "Seriously. I told them yes. But on my terms. Real food. Real people. No glitter sprinkles unless *I* say so."

He laughed. A real one, low and warm and just a little disbelieving.

They sat in silence for another beat. Then Eli reached into his jacket pocket and pulled out something small and folded. He handed it to her like a secret.

It was a napkin — slightly creased, stained with what might've been fig jam — and on it was a rough sketch. A floorplan. Tables. An open kitchen. A space filled with light and people. Scribbled in the corner: *Holiday Pop-Up? Traveling?*

"I was thinking we do it… together," he said, a little gruffly, like the idea was almost too fragile to speak aloud.

Claire looked down at the drawing, her heart rising in her chest like it was full of whipped cream and wonder. "Only if I get naming rights."

He raised a brow. "Pumpkin Spice & Sass?"

"Tempting," she said, tapping the napkin, "but I was thinking... *The Thankful Table.*"

He considered. Then nodded. "That's good. That's... really good."

They were back in Eli's kitchen by late afternoon, where the counters were still dusted with remnants of the festival, and Claire was piping whipped cream onto pumpkin pancakes "for content," even though the camera wasn't rolling.

Eli walked by, dipped a finger in the cream, and smudged it gently on the tip of her nose.

Claire gasped. "You did not."

"Oops," he said, utterly unrepentant.

She retaliated by smearing whipped cream across his cheek, and he pulled her toward him, catching her laughter in a kiss that was flirty and soft and sticky with sugar. Her fingers curled in the hem of his shirt. His hands found her waist. And somewhere in the background, the timer on the oven dinged and was completely ignored.

When they finally pulled apart, Claire leaned against the counter, cheeks pink, hair askew, and heart more full than it had ever been.

Eli brushed a stray curl from her cheek, still grinning. "Second helpings never tasted this good."

And Claire, who had once thought she needed the big city and the spotlight to feel like she mattered, looked at him — flour-dusted, grinning, a little bit whipped-cream-kissed — and realized she'd already found everything she needed.

Right here.

In this kitchen.

In this town.

With *him*.

CHAPTER 16
THANKFUL HEARTS

Some love stories don't end with fireworks. They end with cinnamon in the air, hands held beneath falling leaves, and the soft, golden hush of *belonging*.

One year later, **Harvest Hollow** had become something more than quaint — it had become a destination. The second annual *Thanksgiving Festival* had drawn twice as many visitors, and this time, there were no wrestling matches or rainstorms, just clear skies and cobblestone streets wrapped in garlands of marigolds, dried oranges, and tiny lights that flickered like candle flames. The town was alive with music and laughter, smells of roasted squash and fresh bread curling out of every doorway.

And at the center of it all stood the two people who had once tried very hard *not* to fall in love.

Claire Monroe moved through the crowd in a burnt-orange sweater and an apron that said *Whip It Good*, holding a mixing bowl in one arm and a microphone in the other. She was filming a fall dessert segment with a cluster of kids around her, all covered in sprinkles and giggles, each holding their own "Claire-style mini pie."

Nearby, a camera operator tracked her movements like she was a celebrity — which, in this little town, she was.

Across the square, Eli Hunter was teaching a cooking class to a group of teens inside the community center. His sleeves were rolled up, his hair dusted in flour, and his patience somehow limitless as one kid tried to flambé sweet potatoes and nearly singed his eyebrows. When the class clapped at the end, Eli actually smiled — not the half-smirk of a reluctant participant, but a full, heart-deep smile that made Claire pause mid-sentence just to watch him.

At the lantern arch — now a permanent fixture in the square — Lucy was officiating a *Friendsgiving Wedding*. Two brides in flannel held hands and laughed through their vows as lanterns floated into the sky behind them. There were no pews. Just hay bales, cider, and happy tears.

This town, Claire thought, this life... this was the kind of love that lasted. Not the kind you chased — the kind you built. One pie. One lantern. One whispered promise at a time.

That night, the tables inside Eli's restaurant were full — friends, neighbors, volunteers, and strangers who felt like neither. The air was warm with food and stories, the windows fogged with breath and laughter. At the head of the main table sat Claire and Eli, shoulder to shoulder, their hands intertwined beneath the linen. Claire had spent most of the afternoon pretending she wasn't crying every five minutes, and Eli had spent most of the evening pretending he wasn't watching her more than his own plate.

Then came dessert.

Mini pumpkin pies, perfect and glowing in the candlelight. Claire lifted her fork to take a bite when her spoon clinked against something unexpected.

She paused. Frowned. And then, very carefully, pulled a small silver ring from the center of the pie. Her breath caught.

Eli stood.

Everyone went quiet.

"I had a whole speech planned," he said, cheeks flushed red, "but

I forgot every word the second you walked in here in that ridiculous apron and made me fall for you again."

Claire laughed — breathless and already crying.

"You're the best recipe I've ever stumbled into," he said, kneeling beside her chair, ring in hand, eyes shining. "And I don't want another bite of life without you. So... will you marry me?"

She didn't wait.

"Only if we do the stuffing your way this year," she whispered, eyes glistening, voice trembling with joy.

Eli smiled, slipping the ring onto her flour-dusted finger. "Deal."

They kissed under the twinkling lights of the lantern arch, while the town erupted into applause and confetti made of dried herbs and love notes rained from above — Lucy's idea, naturally.

Later that night, as the square filled for the final lantern launch, the whole town gathered under the lights for a photo. Babies were passed to grandparents, mugs raised high, arms slung around shoulders. Someone counted down.

Claire stood between Eli and Lucy, one hand on her heart, the other tangled in Eli's fingers, and as the lights flashed and the lanterns soared, her voice rose in a soft narration meant just for the moment, and maybe for the rest of her life.

"Turns out, love was the secret ingredient all along."

And beneath the glow of floating light and full hearts, it was true. Every word of it.

Because here — in this town, with these people, and with him — Claire Monroe had finally found her forever recipe.

And it was perfect.

Just like pie.

CHAPTER 17
THANK YOU FOR READING!

Thankful Hearts and Pumpkin Spice Kisses made you smile, swoon, or believe in second chances again, I'd be so grateful if you left a short review. Your words help new readers find the story—and help me keep writing love stories filled with warmth, heart, and a little bit of glitter.

www.ingramcontent.com/pod-product-compliance
Lightning Source LLC
LaVergne TN
LVHW050026080526
838202LV00069B/6927